P9-CFF-534

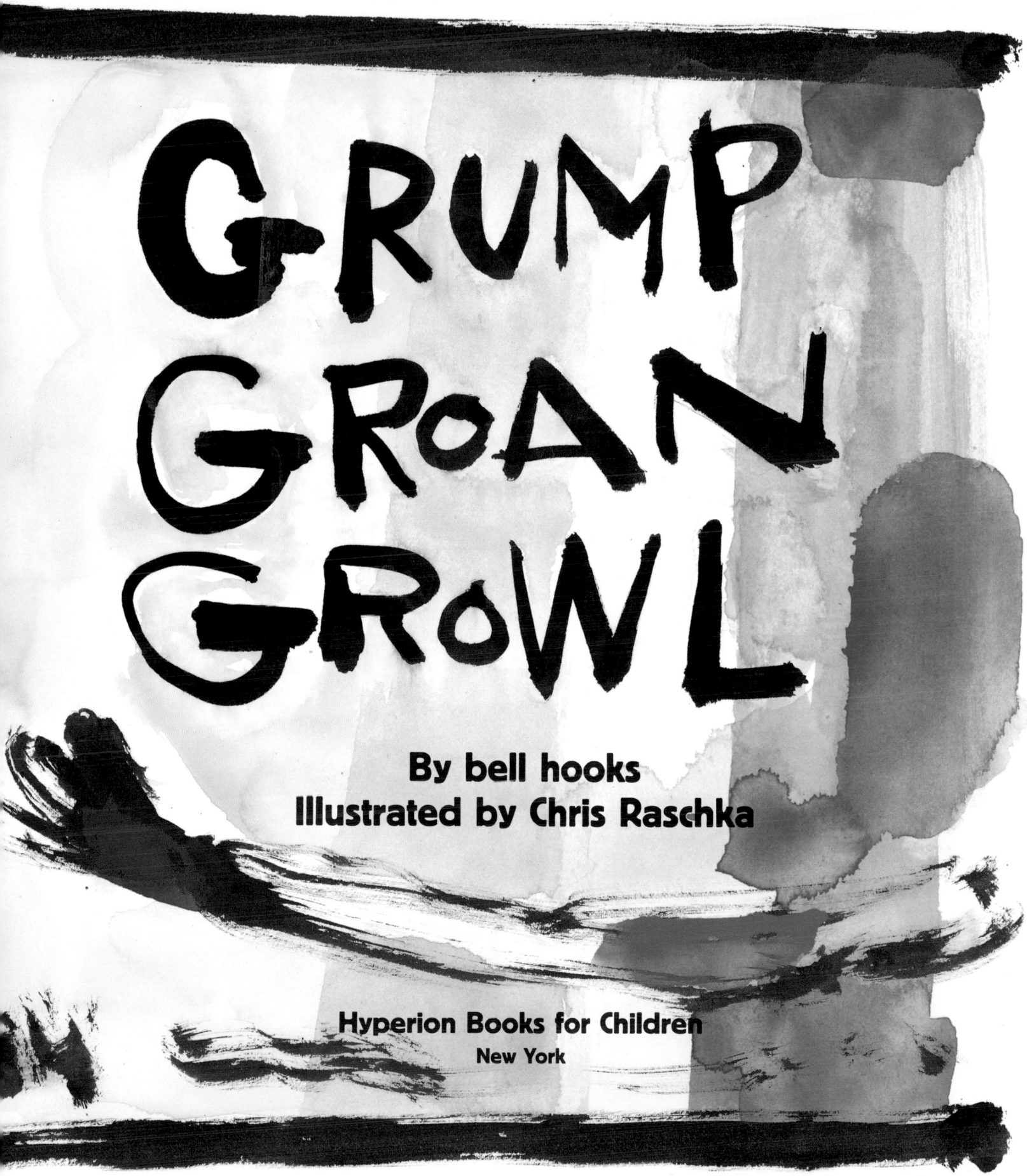

By bell hooks
Illustrated by Chris Raschka

Hyperion Books for Children
New York

Text copyright © 2008 by bell hooks
Illustrations copyright © 2008 by Chris Raschka

All rights reserved. Published by Hyperion Books for Children, an imprint of Disney Book Group. No part of this book may be reproduced or transmitted in any form or by any means, electronic or mechanical, including photocopying, recording, or by any information storage and retrieval system, without written permission from the publisher. For information address Hyperion Books for Children, 114 Fifth Avenue, New York, New York 10011-5690.

Printed in Hong Kong
First Edition
1 3 5 7 9 10 8 6 4 2
Library of Congress Cataloging-in-Publication Data on file.
ISBN-13: 978-0-7868-0816-8
ISBN-10: 0-7868-0816-0
Reinforced binding
Visit www.hyperionbooksforchildren.com

for MARCUS
best boy–
beloved reader
–bh
For bell
–CR

GRUMP

GROAN

GROWL

BAD

MooD
on the prowl

CAN'T
STAND
OUTSIDE

CAN'T

HIDE

RUMP
ROAN
ROWL

ALL I AM IS

WILD

CAN'T FLEE

CAN'T GO AWAY

GRUMP
GROAN
GROWL

BAD MOOD
on the PROWL

JUST GO
IN

SIDE

No need to hide

Just let those
feelings
BE

JUST LET THEM

PASS

JUST GO
INSIDE

Just
let
it

bide